Dear Parent:
Your child's love of reading starts here!

Every child learns to read in a different way and at his or her own speed. Some go back and forth between reading levels and read favorite books again and again. Others read through each level in order. You can help your young reader improve and become more confident by encouraging his or her own interests and abilities. From books your child reads with you to the first books he or she reads alone, there are I Can Read Books for every stage of reading:

SHARED READING
Basic language, word repetition, and whimsical illustrations, ideal for sharing with your emergent reader

BEGINNING READING
Short sentences, familiar words, and simple concepts for children eager to read on their own

READING WITH HELP
Engaging stories, longer sentences, and language play for developing readers

READING ALONE
Complex plots, challenging vocabulary, and high-interest topics for the independent reader

I Can Read Books have introduced children to the joy of reading since 1957. Featuring award-winning authors and illustrators and a fabulous cast of beloved characters, I Can Read Books set the standard for beginning readers.

A lifetime of discovery begins with the magical words "I Can Read!"

Visit www.icanread.com for information
on enriching your child's reading experience.

For Will, who would just
use a ladder

Balzer + Bray is an imprint of HarperCollins Publishers.
I Can Read® and I Can Read Book® are trademarks of HarperCollins Publishers.

Library of Congress Control Number: 2022036196
ISBN 978-0-06-327791-5 (trade bdg.) — ISBN 978-0-06-327792-2 (pbk.)

The artist used pencil, colored pencil, and watercolor, assembled digitally, to create the illustrations for this
book.
Typography by Dana Fritts
Title hand lettering by Alexandra Snowdon

23 24 25 26 27   LB   10 9 8 7 6 5 4 3 2 1   First Edition

FOX

Has a

PROBLEM

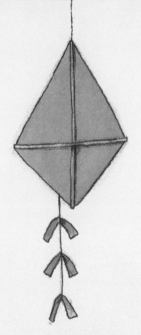

Corey R. Tabor

BALZER + BRAY

An Imprint of HarperCollinsPublishers

Fox has a problem.

It is not a new problem.

But Fox has an idea.

A big idea.

WHIRRRR

Now Bear has a problem.

A very new problem.

But Fox has another idea.

Another big idea.

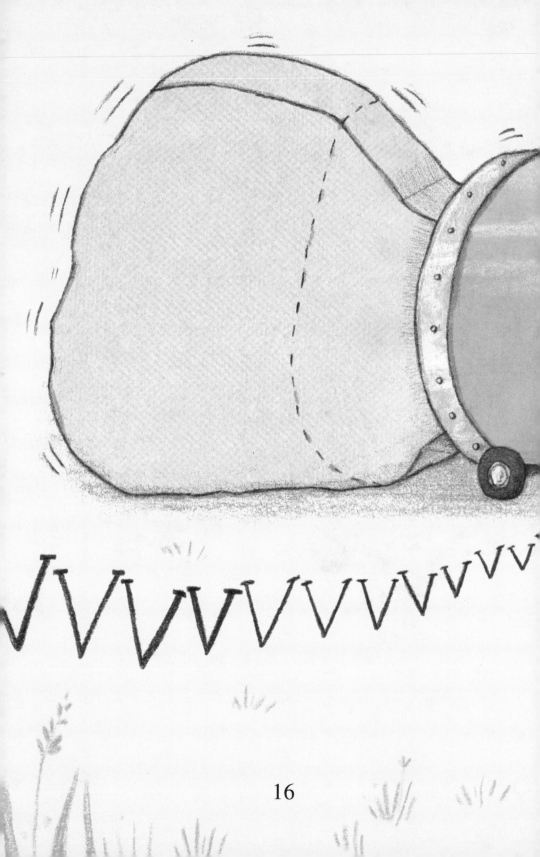

BONK!

Now Rabbit has a problem.

A very new, very big problem.

But Fox has an idea.

A sharp idea.

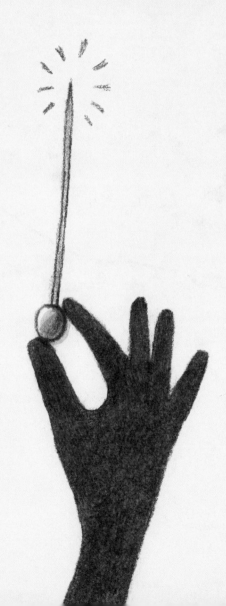

The animals have a problem.

The animals have a fox problem.

"WAIT!" says Elephant.

Elephant has an idea.

It is a very good idea.